# Always

## Ann Stott

illustrated by Matt Phelan

SCHOLASTIC INC.
New York  Toronto  London  Auckland  Sydney
Mexico City  New Delhi  Hong Kong  Buenos Aires

D1165080

Do you love me?

# Do you love me when

# I get dressed all by myself?

Do you love me when
I'm gentle?

Do you love me when
I'm not?

Do you love me when

I jump in puddles

For Caleb and Quin
A. S.

For my mom
M. P.

ISBN-13: 978-0-545-15900-5
ISBN-10: 0-545-15900-8

Text copyright © 2008 by Ann Stott. Illustrations copyright © 2008 by Matt Phelan. All rights reserved. Published by Scholastic Inc., 557 Broadway, New York, NY 10012, by arrangement with Candlewick Press. SCHOLASTIC and associated logos are trademarks and/or registered trademarks of Scholastic Inc.

12 11 10 9 8 7 6 5 4 3 2                    12 13 14/0

Printed in Singapore                    46

First Scholastic printing, April 2009

This book was typeset in Avril.
The illustrations were done in watercolor.